For children, everywhere

Copyright © 1989 by Peter Haswell

First published in Great Britain 1989
by Walker Books Ltd., London
First American edition 1989

Orchard Books
A division of Franklin Watts, Inc.
387 Park Avenue South
New York, NY 10016

Printed by South China Printing Co., Hong Kong

10 9 8 7 6 5 4 3 2 1

Library of Congress Cataloging-in-Publication Data
Haswell, Peter.
Pog/Peter Haswell.
p.   cm.
Summary: Relates, in simple text and illustrations, the
adventures of an inquisitive pig named Pog.
ISBN 0-531-05843-3.—ISBN 0-531-08443-4 (lib. bdg.)
[1. Pigs—Fiction.] I. Title.
PZ7.H2815Po   1989   88-34466
[E]—dc19   CIP
                                      AC

The text of this book is set in Veronan.

POG

Written and illustrated by
Peter Haswell

Orchard Books
A Division of Franklin Watts, Inc.
New York

Pog Looked

Pog looked in the mirror.

"That's not me," he said.

Pog walked around the house.

Then he walked back.

Pog looked in the mirror again.

"I suppose," he said, "it could be me."

Pog walked around the house again.

He looked in the mirror once more.

"No," he said. "It's not me."

Pog sat down and thought.

"It definitely wasn't me," he said.

"But if it wasn't me . . ."

"Who was it?"

Pog Found

Pog found a banana.
"I wonder what a
banana does," said Pog.

He put it on his head.

It fell off.

He dropped it on the floor.

It didn't bounce.

He put it in a vase. 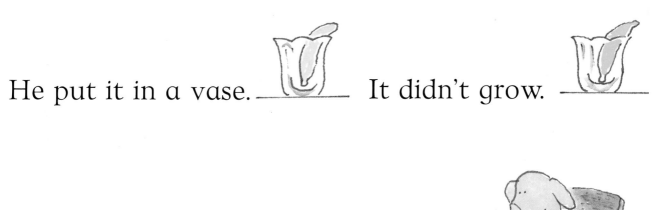 It didn't grow.

Pog peeled the banana.

He threw away the skin.

Pog walked . . .

"Now I know what
a banana does."

"It makes you fall down!"

Pog Walked

Pog walked in the park.

He was hot.

Pog saw the pond.

He dived in.

Now he was cool.

But he was wet.

Pog walked in the park again.

Now he was dry  but hot.

 He saw the pond again.

He jumped in.

Now he was cool but wet.

 Pog walked out of the park.

"This park's no good," he said.

"It's too hot and wet!"

Pog Painted

Pog painted the ceiling red.

He painted the wall red.

He painted the floor red.

He painted the fireplace red.

Pog painted the chair red.

 He painted his boots red.

He painted his feet red.

Pog said, "I don't know why I did all that. . . ."

"I don't like red!"

Pog Smelled

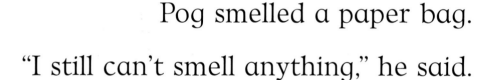

Pog smelled a cucumber.

"I can't smell anything," he said.

Pog smelled a paper bag.

"I still can't smell anything," he said.

Pog smelled a telephone.

"No. I can't smell anything."

Pog smelled a piano.

"No smell," he said.

Pog smelled a ceiling.

"Not a thing," he said.

"The problem is my nose.

It sniffs and blows . . ."

"but I can't get it to smell!"

Pog Dug

Pog dug and dug.  He dug a hole.

 Pog stood in the hole.

He sat in the hole.

 Pog decided to take the hole home.

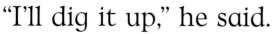

"I'll dig it up," he said.

 Pog dug again.

He dug  and dug.

Then Pog tried to pick the hole up.

 He tried and tried.

 Pog gave up.

"I'll just have to leave this hole," he said.

"I've made it too big and heavy!"

Pog Hid

Pog hid under the table.

"They could find me here," he said.

Pog hid behind the curtains.

"They could find me here, too."

Pog hid in the cupboard.

"They just might find me here."

Pog hid behind the door.

"They'll probably find me here."

Pog hid under the bed.

"They're sure to find me here."

Pog thought for a while.

Then . . .

Pog shut his eyes.
"Now they'll never
find me," he said.

But they did.

"We missed you, Pog!"